# Tears, Idle Tears

## And

## Other Poems

Alfred Lord Tennyson

© 2023 Culturea Editions
Texte et illustration de couverture : © domaine public
Edition : Culturea (Hérault, 34)
Contact : infos@culturea.fr
Retrouvez notre catalogue sur http://culturea.fr
Imprimé en Allemagne par Books on Demand
Design typographique : Derek Murphy
Layout : Reedsy (https://reedsy.com/)
ISBN : 9791041817887
Dépôt légal : Juin 2023

## Tears, Idle Tears

Tears, idle tears, I know not what they mean,
Tears from the depth of some divine despair
Rise in the heart, and gather to the eyes,
In looking on the happy Autumn-fields,
And thinking of the days that are no more.

Fresh as the first beam glittering on a sail,
That brings our friends up from the underworld,
Sad as the last which reddens over one
That sinks with all we love below the verge;
So sad, so fresh, the days that are no more.

Ah, sad and strange as in dark summer dawns
The earliest pipe of half-awakened birds
To dying ears, when unto dying eyes
The casement slowly grows a glimmering square;
So sad, so strange, the days that are no more.

Dear as remembered kisses after death,
And sweet as those by hopeless fancy feigned
On lips that are for others; deep as love,
Deep as first love, and wild with all regret;
O Death in Life, the days that are no more!

## The Brook

I come from haunts of coot and hern,
I make a sudden sally
And sparkle out among the fern,
To bicker down a valley.

By thirty hills I hurry down,
Or slip between the ridges,
By twenty thorpes, a little town,
And half a hundred bridges.

Till last by Philip's farm I flow
To join the brimming river,
For men may come and men may go,

But I go on for ever.

I chatter over stony ways,
In little sharps and trebles,
I bubble into eddying bays,
I babble on the pebbles.

With many a curve my banks I fret
By many a field and fallow,
And many a fairy foreland set
With willow-weed and mallow.

I chatter, chatter, as I flow
To join the brimming river,
For men may come and men may go,
But I go on for ever.

I wind about, and in and out,
With here a blossom sailing,
And here and there a lusty trout,
And here and there a grayling,

And here and there a foamy flake
Upon me, as I travel
With many a silvery waterbreak
Above the golden gravel,

And draw them all along, and flow
To join the brimming river
For men may come and men may go,
But I go on for ever.

I steal by lawns and grassy plots,
I slide by hazel covers;
I move the sweet forget-me-nots
That grow for happy lovers.

I slip, I slide, I gloom, I glance,
Among my skimming swallows;
I make the netted sunbeam dance

Against my sandy shallows.

I murmur under moon and stars
In brambly wildernesses;
I linger by my shingly bars;
I loiter round my cresses;

And out again I curve and flow
To join the brimming river,
For men may come and men may go,
But I go on for ever.

**The Coming Of Arthur**

Leodogran, the King of Cameliard,
Had one fair daughter, and none other child;
And she was the fairest of all flesh on earth,
Guinevere, and in her his one delight.

For many a petty king ere Arthur came
Ruled in this isle, and ever waging war
Each upon other, wasted all the land;
And still from time to time the heathen host
Swarmed overseas, and harried what was left.
And so there grew great tracts of wilderness,
Wherein the beast was ever more and more,
But man was less and less, till Arthur came.
For first Aurelius lived and fought and died,
And after him King Uther fought and died,
But either failed to make the kingdom one.
And after these King Arthur for a space,
And through the puissance of his Table Round,
Drew all their petty princedoms under him.
Their king and head, and made a realm, and reigned.

And thus the land of Cameliard was waste,
Thick with wet woods, and many a beast therein,
And none or few to scare or chase the beast;
So that wild dog, and wolf and boar and bear
Came night and day, and rooted in the fields,
And wallowed in the gardens of the King.

And ever and anon the wolf would steal
The children and devour, but now and then,
Her own brood lost or dead, lent her fierce teat
To human sucklings; and the children, housed
In her foul den, there at their meat would growl,
And mock their foster mother on four feet,
Till, straightened, they grew up to wolf-like men,
Worse than the wolves. And King Leodogran
Groaned for the Roman legions here again,
And Csar's eagle: then his brother king,
Urien, assailed him: last a heathen horde,
Reddening the sun with smoke and earth with blood,
And on the spike that split the mother's heart
Spitting the child, brake on him, till, amazed,
He knew not whither he should turn for aid.

But--for he heard of Arthur newly crowned,
Though not without an uproar made by those
Who cried, `He is not Uther's son'--the King
Sent to him, saying, `Arise, and help us thou!
For here between the man and beast we die.'

And Arthur yet had done no deed of arms,
But heard the call, and came: and Guinevere
Stood by the castle walls to watch him pass;
But since he neither wore on helm or shield
The golden symbol of his kinglihood,
But rode a simple knight among his knights,
And many of these in richer arms than he,
She saw him not, or marked not, if she saw,
One among many, though his face was bare.
But Arthur, looking downward as he past,
Felt the light of her eyes into his life
Smite on the sudden, yet rode on, and pitched
His tents beside the forest. Then he drave
The heathen; after, slew the beast, and felled
The forest, letting in the sun, and made
Broad pathways for the hunter and the knight
And so returned.

For while he lingered there,
A doubt that ever smouldered in the hearts
Of those great Lords and Barons of his realm
Flashed forth and into war: for most of these,
Colleaguing with a score of petty kings,
Made head against him, crying, `Who is he
That he should rule us? who hath proven him
King Uther's son? for lo! we look at him,
And find nor face nor bearing, limbs nor voice,
Are like to those of Uther whom we knew.
This is the son of Gorlos, not the King;
This is the son of Anton, not the King.'

And Arthur, passing thence to battle, felt
Travail, and throes and agonies of the life,
Desiring to be joined with Guinevere;
And thinking as he rode, `Her father said
That there between the man and beast they die.
Shall I not lift her from this land of beasts
Up to my throne, and side by side with me?
What happiness to reign a lonely king,
Vext--O ye stars that shudder over me,
O earth that soundest hollow under me,
Vext with waste dreams? for saving I be joined
To her that is the fairest under heaven,
I seem as nothing in the mighty world,
And cannot will my will, nor work my work
Wholly, nor make myself in mine own realm
Victor and lord. But were I joined with her,
Then might we live together as one life,
And reigning with one will in everything
Have power on this dark land to lighten it,
And power on this dead world to make it live.'

Thereafter--as he speaks who tells the tale--
When Arthur reached a field-of-battle bright
With pitched pavilions of his foe, the world
Was all so clear about him, that he saw
The smallest rock far on the faintest hill,
And even in high day the morning star.

So when the King had set his banner broad,
At once from either side, with trumpet-blast,
And shouts, and clarions shrilling unto blood,
The long-lanced battle let their horses run.
And now the Barons and the kings prevailed,
And now the King, as here and there that war
Went swaying; but the Powers who walk the world
Made lightnings and great thunders over him,
And dazed all eyes, till Arthur by main might,
And mightier of his hands with every blow,
And leading all his knighthood threw the kings
Cardos, Urien, Cradlemont of Wales,
Claudias, and Clariance of Northumberland,
The King Brandagoras of Latangor,
With Anguisant of Erin, Morganore,
And Lot of Orkney. Then, before a voice
As dreadful as the shout of one who sees
To one who sins, and deems himself alone
And all the world asleep, they swerved and brake
Flying, and Arthur called to stay the brands
That hacked among the flyers, `Ho! they yield!'
So like a painted battle the war stood
Silenced, the living quiet as the dead,
And in the heart of Arthur joy was lord.
He laughed upon his warrior whom he loved
And honoured most. `Thou dost not doubt me King,
So well thine arm hath wrought for me today.'
`Sir and my liege,' he cried, `the fire of God
Descends upon thee in the battle-field:
I know thee for my King!' Whereat the two,
For each had warded either in the fight,
Sware on the field of death a deathless love.
And Arthur said, `Man's word is God in man:
Let chance what will, I trust thee to the death.'

Then quickly from the foughten field he sent
Ulfius, and Brastias, and Bedivere,
His new-made knights, to King Leodogran,
Saying, `If I in aught have served thee well,
Give me thy daughter Guinevere to wife.'

Whom when he heard, Leodogran in heart
Debating--`How should I that am a king,
However much he holp me at my need,
Give my one daughter saving to a king,
And a king's son?'--lifted his voice, and called
A hoary man, his chamberlain, to whom
He trusted all things, and of him required
His counsel: `Knowest thou aught of Arthur's birth?'

Then spake the hoary chamberlain and said,
`Sir King, there be but two old men that know:
And each is twice as old as I; and one
Is Merlin, the wise man that ever served
King Uther through his magic art; and one
Is Merlin's master (so they call him) Bleys,
Who taught him magic, but the scholar ran
Before the master, and so far, that Bleys,
Laid magic by, and sat him down, and wrote
All things and whatsoever Merlin did
In one great annal-book, where after-years
Will learn the secret of our Arthur's birth.'

To whom the King Leodogran replied,
`O friend, had I been holpen half as well
By this King Arthur as by thee today,
Then beast and man had had their share of me:
But summon here before us yet once more
Ulfius, and Brastias, and Bedivere.'

Then, when they came before him, the King said,
`I have seen the cuckoo chased by lesser fowl,
And reason in the chase: but wherefore now
Do these your lords stir up the heat of war,
Some calling Arthur born of Gorlos,
Others of Anton? Tell me, ye yourselves,
Hold ye this Arthur for King Uther's son?'

And Ulfius and Brastias answered, `Ay.'
Then Bedivere, the first of all his knights

Knighted by Arthur at his crowning, spake--
For bold in heart and act and word was he,
Whenever slander breathed against the King--

`Sir, there be many rumours on this head:
For there be those who hate him in their hearts,
Call him baseborn, and since his ways are sweet,
And theirs are bestial, hold him less than man:
And there be those who deem him more than man,
And dream he dropt from heaven: but my belief
In all this matter--so ye care to learn--
Sir, for ye know that in King Uther's time
The prince and warrior Gorlos, he that held
Tintagil castle by the Cornish sea,
Was wedded with a winsome wife, Ygerne:
And daughters had she borne him,--one whereof,
Lot's wife, the Queen of Orkney, Bellicent,
Hath ever like a loyal sister cleaved
To Arthur,--but a son she had not borne.
And Uther cast upon her eyes of love:
But she, a stainless wife to Gorlos,
So loathed the bright dishonour of his love,
That Gorlos and King Uther went to war:
And overthrown was Gorlos and slain.
Then Uther in his wrath and heat besieged
Ygerne within Tintagil, where her men,
Seeing the mighty swarm about their walls,
Left her and fled, and Uther entered in,
And there was none to call to but himself.
So, compassed by the power of the King,
Enforced was she to wed him in her tears,
And with a shameful swiftness: afterward,
Not many moons, King Uther died himself,
Moaning and wailing for an heir to rule
After him, lest the realm should go to wrack.
And that same night, the night of the new year,
By reason of the bitterness and grief
That vext his mother, all before his time
Was Arthur born, and all as soon as born
Delivered at a secret postern-gate

To Merlin, to be holden far apart
Until his hour should come; because the lords
Of that fierce day were as the lords of this,
Wild beasts, and surely would have torn the child
Piecemeal among them, had they known; for each
But sought to rule for his own self and hand,
And many hated Uther for the sake
Of Gorlos. Wherefore Merlin took the child,
And gave him to Sir Anton, an old knight
And ancient friend of Uther; and his wife
Nursed the young prince, and reared him with her own;
And no man knew. And ever since the lords
Have foughten like wild beasts among themselves,
So that the realm has gone to wrack: but now,
This year, when Merlin (for his hour had come)
Brought Arthur forth, and set him in the hall,
Proclaiming, "Here is Uther's heir, your king,"
A hundred voices cried, "Away with him!
No king of ours! a son of Gorlos he,
Or else the child of Anton, and no king,
Or else baseborn." Yet Merlin through his craft,
And while the people clamoured for a king,
Had Arthur crowned; but after, the great lords
Banded, and so brake out in open war.'

Then while the King debated with himself
If Arthur were the child of shamefulness,
Or born the son of Gorlos, after death,
Or Uther's son, and born before his time,
Or whether there were truth in anything
Said by these three, there came to Cameliard,
With Gawain and young Modred, her two sons,
Lot's wife, the Queen of Orkney, Bellicent;
Whom as he could, not as he would, the King
Made feast for, saying, as they sat at meat,

`A doubtful throne is ice on summer seas.
Ye come from Arthur's court. Victor his men
Report him! Yea, but ye--think ye this king--
So many those that hate him, and so strong,

So few his knights, however brave they be--
Hath body enow to hold his foemen down?'

`O King,' she cried, `and I will tell thee: few,
Few, but all brave, all of one mind with him;
For I was near him when the savage yells
Of Uther's peerage died, and Arthur sat
Crowned on the das, and his warriors cried,
"Be thou the king, and we will work thy will
Who love thee." Then the King in low deep tones,
And simple words of great authority,
Bound them by so strait vows to his own self,
That when they rose, knighted from kneeling, some
Were pale as at the passing of a ghost,
Some flushed, and others dazed, as one who wakes
Half-blinded at the coming of a light.

`But when he spake and cheered his Table Round
With large, divine, and comfortable words,
Beyond my tongue to tell thee--I beheld
From eye to eye through all their Order flash
A momentary likeness of the King:
And ere it left their faces, through the cross
And those around it and the Crucified,
Down from the casement over Arthur, smote
Flame-colour, vert and azure, in three rays,
One falling upon each of three fair queens,
Who stood in silence near his throne, the friends
Of Arthur, gazing on him, tall, with bright
Sweet faces, who will help him at his need.

`And there I saw mage Merlin, whose vast wit
And hundred winters are but as the hands
Of loyal vassals toiling for their liege.

`And near him stood the Lady of the Lake,
Who knows a subtler magic than his own--
Clothed in white samite, mystic, wonderful.
She gave the King his huge cross-hilted sword,
Whereby to drive the heathen out: a mist

Of incense curled about her, and her face
Wellnigh was hidden in the minster gloom;
But there was heard among the holy hymns
A voice as of the waters, for she dwells
Down in a deep; calm, whatsoever storms
May shake the world, and when the surface rolls,
Hath power to walk the waters like our Lord.

`There likewise I beheld Excalibur
Before him at his crowning borne, the sword
That rose from out the bosom of the lake,
And Arthur rowed across and took it--rich
With jewels, elfin Urim, on the hilt,
Bewildering heart and eye--the blade so bright
That men are blinded by it--on one side,
Graven in the oldest tongue of all this world,
"Take me," but turn the blade and ye shall see,
And written in the speech ye speak yourself,
"Cast me away!" And sad was Arthur's face
Taking it, but old Merlin counselled him,
"Take thou and strike! the time to cast away
Is yet far-off." So this great brand the king
Took, and by this will beat his foemen down.'

Thereat Leodogran rejoiced, but thought
To sift his doubtings to the last, and asked,
Fixing full eyes of question on her face,
`The swallow and the swift are near akin,
But thou art closer to this noble prince,
Being his own dear sister;' and she said,
`Daughter of Gorlos and Ygerne am I;'
`And therefore Arthur's sister?' asked the King.
She answered, `These be secret things,' and signed
To those two sons to pass, and let them be.
And Gawain went, and breaking into song
Sprang out, and followed by his flying hair
Ran like a colt, and leapt at all he saw:
But Modred laid his ear beside the doors,
And there half-heard; the same that afterward
Struck for the throne, and striking found his doom.

And then the Queen made answer, `What know I?
For dark my mother was in eyes and hair,
And dark in hair and eyes am I; and dark
Was Gorlos, yea and dark was Uther too,
Wellnigh to blackness; but this King is fair
Beyond the race of Britons and of men.
Moreover, always in my mind I hear
A cry from out the dawning of my life,
A mother weeping, and I hear her say,
"O that ye had some brother, pretty one,
To guard thee on the rough ways of the world."'

`Ay,' said the King, `and hear ye such a cry?
But when did Arthur chance upon thee first?'

`O King!' she cried, `and I will tell thee true:
He found me first when yet a little maid:
Beaten I had been for a little fault
Whereof I was not guilty; and out I ran
And flung myself down on a bank of heath,
And hated this fair world and all therein,
And wept, and wished that I were dead; and he--
I know not whether of himself he came,
Or brought by Merlin, who, they say, can walk
Unseen at pleasure--he was at my side,
And spake sweet words, and comforted my heart,
And dried my tears, being a child with me.
And many a time he came, and evermore
As I grew greater grew with me; and sad
At times he seemed, and sad with him was I,
Stern too at times, and then I loved him not,
But sweet again, and then I loved him well.
And now of late I see him less and less,
But those first days had golden hours for me,
For then I surely thought he would be king.

`But let me tell thee now another tale:
For Bleys, our Merlin's master, as they say,
Died but of late, and sent his cry to me,

To hear him speak before he left his life.
Shrunk like a fairy changeling lay the mage;
And when I entered told me that himself
And Merlin ever served about the King,
Uther, before he died; and on the night
When Uther in Tintagil past away
Moaning and wailing for an heir, the two
Left the still King, and passing forth to breathe,
Then from the castle gateway by the chasm
Descending through the dismal night--a night
In which the bounds of heaven and earth were lost--
Beheld, so high upon the dreary deeps
It seemed in heaven, a ship, the shape thereof
A dragon winged, and all from stern to stern
Bright with a shining people on the decks,
And gone as soon as seen. And then the two
Dropt to the cove, and watched the great sea fall,
Wave after wave, each mightier than the last,
Till last, a ninth one, gathering half the deep
And full of voices, slowly rose and plunged
Roaring, and all the wave was in a flame:
And down the wave and in the flame was borne
A naked babe, and rode to Merlin's feet,
Who stoopt and caught the babe, and cried "The King!
Here is an heir for Uther!" And the fringe
Of that great breaker, sweeping up the strand,
Lashed at the wizard as he spake the word,
And all at once all round him rose in fire,
So that the child and he were clothed in fire.
And presently thereafter followed calm,
Free sky and stars: "And this the same child," he said,
"Is he who reigns; nor could I part in peace
Till this were told." And saying this the seer
Went through the strait and dreadful pass of death,
Not ever to be questioned any more
Save on the further side; but when I met
Merlin, and asked him if these things were truth--
The shining dragon and the naked child
Descending in the glory of the seas--
He laughed as is his wont, and answered me

In riddling triplets of old time, and said:

`"Rain, rain, and sun! a rainbow in the sky!
A young man will be wiser by and by;
An old man's wit may wander ere he die.
Rain, rain, and sun! a rainbow on the lea!
And truth is this to me, and that to thee;
And truth or clothed or naked let it be.
Rain, sun, and rain! and the free blossom blows:
Sun, rain, and sun! and where is he who knows?
From the great deep to the great deep he goes."

`So Merlin riddling angered me; but thou
Fear not to give this King thy only child,
Guinevere: so great bards of him will sing
Hereafter; and dark sayings from of old
Ranging and ringing through the minds of men,
And echoed by old folk beside their fires
For comfort after their wage-work is done,
Speak of the King; and Merlin in our time
Hath spoken also, not in jest, and sworn
Though men may wound him that he will not die,
But pass, again to come; and then or now
Utterly smite the heathen underfoot,
Till these and all men hail him for their king.'

She spake and King Leodogran rejoiced,
But musing, `Shall I answer yea or nay?'
Doubted, and drowsed, nodded and slept, and saw,
Dreaming, a slope of land that ever grew,
Field after field, up to a height, the peak
Haze-hidden, and thereon a phantom king,
Now looming, and now lost; and on the slope
The sword rose, the hind fell, the herd was driven,
Fire glimpsed; and all the land from roof and rick,
In drifts of smoke before a rolling wind,
Streamed to the peak, and mingled with the haze
And made it thicker; while the phantom king
Sent out at times a voice; and here or there
Stood one who pointed toward the voice, the rest

Slew on and burnt, crying, `No king of ours,
No son of Uther, and no king of ours;'
Till with a wink his dream was changed, the haze
Descended, and the solid earth became
As nothing, but the King stood out in heaven,
Crowned. And Leodogran awoke, and sent
Ulfius, and Brastias and Bedivere,
Back to the court of Arthur answering yea.

Then Arthur charged his warrior whom he loved
And honoured most, Sir Lancelot, to ride forth
And bring the Queen;--and watched him from the gates:
And Lancelot past away among the flowers,
(For then was latter April) and returned
Among the flowers, in May, with Guinevere.
To whom arrived, by Dubric the high saint,
Chief of the church in Britain, and before
The stateliest of her altar-shrines, the King
That morn was married, while in stainless white,
The fair beginners of a nobler time,
And glorying in their vows and him, his knights
Stood around him, and rejoicing in his joy.
Far shone the fields of May through open door,
The sacred altar blossomed white with May,
The Sun of May descended on their King,
They gazed on all earth's beauty in their Queen,
Rolled incense, and there past along the hymns
A voice as of the waters, while the two
Sware at the shrine of Christ a deathless love:
And Arthur said, `Behold, thy doom is mine.
Let chance what will, I love thee to the death!'
To whom the Queen replied with drooping eyes,
`King and my lord, I love thee to the death!'
And holy Dubric spread his hands and spake,
`Reign ye, and live and love, and make the world
Other, and may thy Queen be one with thee,
And all this Order of thy Table Round
Fulfil the boundless purpose of their King!'

So Dubric said; but when they left the shrine

Great Lords from Rome before the portal stood,
In scornful stillness gazing as they past;
Then while they paced a city all on fire
With sun and cloth of gold, the trumpets blew,
And Arthur's knighthood sang before the King:--

`Blow, trumpet, for the world is white with May;
Blow trumpet, the long night hath rolled away!
Blow through the living world--"Let the King reign."

`Shall Rome or Heathen rule in Arthur's realm?
Flash brand and lance, fall battleaxe upon helm,
Fall battleaxe, and flash brand! Let the King reign.

`Strike for the King and live! his knights have heard
That God hath told the King a secret word.
Fall battleaxe, and flash brand! Let the King reign.

`Blow trumpet! he will lift us from the dust.
Blow trumpet! live the strength and die the lust!
Clang battleaxe, and clash brand! Let the King reign.

`Strike for the King and die! and if thou diest,
The King is King, and ever wills the highest.
Clang battleaxe, and clash brand! Let the King reign.

`Blow, for our Sun is mighty in his May!
Blow, for our Sun is mightier day by day!
Clang battleaxe, and clash brand! Let the King reign.

`The King will follow Christ, and we the King
In whom high God hath breathed a secret thing.
Fall battleaxe, and flash brand! Let the King reign.'

So sang the knighthood, moving to their hall.
There at the banquet those great Lords from Rome,
The slowly-fading mistress of the world,
Strode in, and claimed their tribute as of yore.
But Arthur spake, `Behold, for these have sworn
To wage my wars, and worship me their King;

The old order changeth, yielding place to new;
And we that fight for our fair father Christ,
Seeing that ye be grown too weak and old
To drive the heathen from your Roman wall,
No tribute will we pay:' so those great lords
Drew back in wrath, and Arthur strove with Rome.

And Arthur and his knighthood for a space
Were all one will, and through that strength the King
Drew in the petty princedoms under him,
Fought, and in twelve great battles overcame
The heathen hordes, and made a realm and reigned.

**The Death of the Old Year**

Full knee-deep lies the winter snow,
And the winter winds are wearily sighing:
Toll ye the church bell sad and slow,
And tread softly and speak low,
For the old year lies a-dying.
Old year you must not die;
You came to us so readily,
You lived with us so steadily,
Old year you shall not die.

He lieth still: he doth not move:
He will not see the dawn of day.
He hath no other life above.
He gave me a friend and a true truelove
And the New-year will take 'em away.
Old year you must not go;
So long you have been with us,
Such joy as you have seen with us,
Old year, you shall not go.

He froth'd his bumpers to the brim;
A jollier year we shall not see.
But tho' his eyes are waxing dim,
And tho' his foes speak ill of him,
He was a friend to me.
Old year, you shall not die;

We did so laugh and cry with you,
I've half a mind to die with you,
Old year, if you must die.

He was full of joke and jest,
But all his merry quips are o'er.
To see him die across the waste
His son and heir doth ride post-haste,
But he'll be dead before.
Every one for his own.
The night is starry and cold, my friend,
And the New-year blithe and bold, my friend,
Comes up to take his own.

How hard he breathes! over the snow
I heard just now the crowing cock.
The shadows flicker to and fro:
The cricket chirps: the light burns low:
'Tis nearly twelve o'clock.
Shake hands, before you die.
Old year, we'll dearly rue for you:
What is it we can do for you?
Speak out before you die.

His face is growing sharp and thin.
Alack! our friend is gone,
Close up his eyes: tie up his chin:
Step from the corpse, and let him in
That standeth there alone,
And waiteth at the door.
There's a new foot on the floor, my friend,
And a new face at the door, my friend,
A new face at the door.

**The Defence of Lucknow**

I
BANNER of England, not for a season, O banner of
Britain, hast thou
Floated in conquering battle or flapt to the battle-
cry!

Never with mightier glory than when we had rear'd thee on high
Flying at top of the roofs in the ghastly siege of Lucknow—
Shot thro' the staff or the halyard, but ever we raised thee anew,
And ever upon the topmost roof our banner of England blew.

II.
Frail were the works that defended the hold that we held with our lives—
Women and children among us, God help them, our children and wives!
Hold it we might—and for fifteen days or for twenty at most.
'Never surrender, I charge you, but every man die at his post!'
Voice of the dead whom we loved, our Lawrence the best of the brave:
Cold were his brows when we kiss'd him—we laid him that night in his grave.
'Every man die at his post!' and there hail'd on our houses and halls
Death from their rifle-bullets, and death from their cannon-balls,
Death in our innermost chamber, and death at our slight barricade,
Death while we stood with the musket, and death while we stoopt to the spade,
Death to the dying, and wounds to the wounded, for often there fell,
Striking the hospital wall, crashing thro' it, their shot and their shell,
Death—for their spies were among us, their marksmen were told of our best,
So that the brute bullet broke thro' the brain that could think for the rest;
Bullets would sing by our foreheads, and bullets would rain at our feet—

Fire from ten thousand at once of the rebels that
girdled us round—
Death at the glimpse of a finger from over the breadth
of a street,
Death from the heights of the mosque and the palace,
and death in the ground!
Mine? yes, a mine! Countermine! down, down! and creep
thro' the hole!
Keep the revolver in hand! you can hear him—the
murderous mole!
Quiet, ah! quiet—wait till the point of the pickaxe be
thro'!
Click with the pick, coming nearer and nearer again
than before—
Now let it speak, and you fire, and the dark pioneer is
no more;
And ever upon the topmost roof our banner of England
blew!

III.
Ay, but the foe sprung his mine many times, and it
chanced on a day
Soon as the blast of that underground thunderclap echo
'd away,
Dark thro' the smoke and the sulphur like so many
fiends in their hell—
Cannon-shot, musket-shot, volley on volley, and yell
upon yell—
Fiercely on all the defences our myriad enemy fell.
What have they done? where is it? Out yonder. Guard the
Redan!
Storm at the Water-gate! storm at the Bailey-gate!
storm, and it ran
Surging and swaying all round us, as ocean on every
side
Plunges and heaves at a bank that is daily devour'd by
the tide—
So many thousands that if they be bold enough, who
shall escape?
Kill or be kill'd, live or die, they shall know we are

soldiers and men
Ready! take aim at their leaders—their masses are
gapp'd with our grape—
Backward they reel like the wave, like the wave
flinging forward again,
Flying and foil'd at the last by the handful they could
not subdue;
And ever upon the topmost roof our banner of England
blew.

IV.
Handful of men as we were, we were English in heart and
in limb,
Strong with the strength of the race to command, to
obey, to endure,
Each of us fought as if hope for the garrison hung but
on him;
Still—could we watch at all points? we were every day
fewer and fewer.
There was a whisper among us, but only a whisper that
past
'Children and wives—if the tigers leap into the fold
unawares—
Every man die at his post—and the foe may outlive us at
last—
Better to fall by the hands that they love, than to
fall into theirs!'
Roar upon roar in a moment two mines by the enemy
sprung
Clove into perilous chasms our walls and our poor
palisades.
Rifleman, true is your heart, but be sure that your
hand be as true!
Sharp is the fire of assault, better aimed are your
flank fusillades—
Twice do we hurl them to earth from the ladders to
which they had clung,
Twice from the ditch where they shelter we drive them
with hand-grenades;
And ever upon the topmost roof our banner of England

blew.

V.
Then on another wild morning another wild earthquake
out-tore
Clean from our lines of defence ten or twelve good
paces or more.
Rifleman, high on the roof, hidden there from the light
of the sun—
One has leapt up on the breach, crying out: 'Follow me,
follow me!'—
Mark him—he falls! then another, and him too, and down
goes he.
Had they been bold enough then, who can tell but the
traitors had won?
Boardings and rafters and doors—an embrasure I make way
for the gun!
Now double-charge it with grape! It is charged and we
fire, and they run.
Praise to our Indian brothers, and let the dark face
have his due!
Thanks to the kindly dark faces who fought with us,
faithful and few,
Fought with the bravest among us, and drove them, and
smote them, and slew,
That ever upon the topmost roof our banner in India
blew.

VI.
Men will forget what we suffer and not what we do. We
can fight!
But to be soldier all day and be sentinel all thro' the
night—
Ever the mine and assault, our sallies, their lying
alarms,
Bugles and drums in the darkness, and shoutings and
soundings to arms,
Ever the labour of fifty that had to be done by five,
Ever the marvel among us that one should be left alive,
Ever the day with its traitorous death from the

loopholes around,
Ever the night with its coffinless corpse to be laid in
the ground,
Heat like the mouth of a hell, or a deluge of cataract
skies,
Stench of old offal decaying, and infinite torment of
flies.
Thoughts of the breezes of May blowing over an English
field,
Cholera, scurvy, and fever, the wound that would not be
heal'd,
Lopping away of the limb by the pitiful-pitiless
knife,—
Torture and trouble in vain,—for it never could save us
a life.
Valour of delicate women who tended the hospital bed,
Horror of women in travail among the dying and dead,
Grief for our perishing children, and never a moment
for grief,
Toil and ineffable weariness, faltering hopes of
relief,
Havelock baffled, or beaten, or butcher'd for all that
we knew—
Then day and night, day and night, coming down on the
still-shatter'd walls
Millions of musket-bullets, and thousands of cannon-
balls—
But ever upon the topmost roof our banner of England
blew.

VII.
Hark cannonade, fusillade! is it true what was told by
the scout,
Outram and Havelock breaking their way through the fell
mutineers?
Surely the pibroch of Europe is ringing again in our
ears!
All on a sudden the garrison utter a jubilant shout,
Havelock's glorious Highlanders answer with conquering
cheers,

Sick from the hospital echo them, women and children
come out,
Blessing the wholesome white faces of Havelock's good
fusileers,
Kissing the war-harden'd hand of the Highlander wet
with their tears!
Dance to the pibroch!—saved! we are saved!—is it you?
is it you?
Saved by the valour of Havelock, saved by the blessing
of Heaven!
'Hold it for fifteen days!' we have held it for eighty-
seven!
And ever aloft on the palace roof the old banner of
England blew.